P9-CLO-966

FIVE GO ON A STRATEGY AWAY DAY

Other adventures in this series:

Five Go Parenting

Five Go Gluten Free

Five on Brexit Island

Five Give Up the Booze

Enid Blyton®

FIVE GO ON A STRATEGY AWAY DAY

Text by

Bruno Vincent

Enid Blyton for Grown-Ups

Quercus

First published in Great Britain in 2016 by

Quercus Editions Ltd
Carmelite House
50 Victoria Embankment
London EC4Y 0DZ

An Hachette UK company

A CIP catalogue record for this book is available
from the British Library

HB ISBN 978 1 78648 224 2
EBOOK ISBN 978 1 78648 225 9

Text by Bruno Vincent
Original illustrations by Eileen A. Soper
Cover illustration by Ruth Palmer

10 9 8 7 6 5 4 3

Typeset by CC Book Production

Printed by GGP Media GmbH, Pößneck

Contents

CHAPTER ONE

Five On a Lovely Railway Journey

'You know, I don't think there's anything I like quite so much as a nice railway journey,' said Anne.

'Woof!' agreed Timmy.

'Mmffffffmnffn,' said a voice.

'What's that, Dick?'

With an effort, Dick managed to remove his face from the armpit of the man in front of him and angle his neck so that he could get a look at Anne. 'I said, once we get to Victoria, perhaps you'll have your wish.'

'Do you *mind*?' came Julian's voice from somewhere in the crush.

'I'm sorry?'

'Would you *please* turn your music down several notches? To merely ear-splitting, perhaps? It's practically making me bleed. You don't see me playing my Melvyn Bragg podcast at full blast to the whole carriage, do you?'

'Happy days,' said George quietly, scratching Timmy

behind the ears. 'Not long to go now, Timmy. Just another eleven stops to Embankment, where we change. God bless the London Underground . . .'

It was not often these days that they all set out on an excursion to the countryside together, and so (despite the threat of sweaty frottage upon the Northern Line) they were excited to be on their way to Victoria to catch a train out of London.

It was several months now since Julian had got a new job for a large multinational corporation called Lupiter Fünckstein at their British headquarters in north London. He had been placed in charge of a large project that was expected to take several years to complete, and, once he arrived, he had realized his team was severely understaffed. He had promptly hired Anne, as she was both well qualified and suited to the role.

He found the experience of being able to tell Anne what to do in a professional context intensely gratifying, so much so that he quickly snapped up Dick as well, and when George's contract with her employer came to an end a few weeks later, her too. Now they had all been working together for almost a month, and so far it had proven to be very harmonious.

'I've always thought of you as a Fatuous Four,' said Barbara.

Today, however, there was a chance that this might change, for it was time for the Annual Lupiter Fünckstein Strategy Away Day (or 'ALFSAD' as George and Dick insisted on referring to it), during which Julian knew he would be expected to show leadership, inspiration and encouragement to the others. There were, however, several impediments to this. First was that he loathed team-building exercises: he fundamentally disagreed with the idea of them; he hated the manner in which they were carried out; he found the measurement of their successes to be entirely dubious and their actual outcomes frequently unhelpful; and, of course, they prevented everyone from getting on with their real work.

What's more, the other three were entering into the thing in a spirit of jolly adventure which filled him with dread. He got the sense that Dick and George felt the same way as he did about team-building exercises, and so were just going to take the piss all day, which would embarrass him professionally. Even worse, Anne seemed genuinely keen.

Added to this, Julian had a hangover. Knowing he wouldn't have any actual work to do today, he had arranged to meet up with some old friends the previous night for a drink, one of those innocent-sounding individual beverages, which had – seemingly of its own accord – expanded into a sprawling binge.

He felt rum, he thought, as the Tube thundered into Embankment station, brakes shrieking. As rum as the three large Captain Morgan-and-Cokes with which he had finished off the previous evening.

'Follow me, please, team!' he called out as they tumbled on to the platform.

Half an hour later, they were taking their seats on the train out of London, and an hour after that, they were at their destination – a small stop in the countryside, from where a cab would take them to the conference centre.

Julian had been trying to keep to himself during the journey, concentrating on his headache, but as they piled into the cab, George squeezed in past him and the plastic bag she was carrying jostled against his knee. He felt the clunking of a four-pack of cans.

'What's in that?' he asked as the cab took off.

'Diet Coke,' George said.

'Rubbish; they don't do Coke in cans that size. That's beer!'

'It's not beer, actually,' George said, refusing to open the bag.

'Cider, then. George, this is not appropriate for a day with colleagues!'

'Oh, take it easy. Everyone feels happier to be part of a team when they've had a couple of pints.'

'Well, do me a favour and hold off having any until lunchtime, at least.'

'That ship may have sailed . . .' muttered Dick.

'Jesus H. Macy. Well, please just don't have any *more* until lunchtime. Can you do that?'

'Of course I can, Mr Stroppy,' said George. 'Sure you don't want one? Hair of the dog?'

Timmy growled at the unfortunate choice of phrase, and George kissed his forehead to apologize.

'*Quite* sure, thank you,' said Julian. 'It'd make me sick. I'm not sure I've even got the stomach for the complimentary glass of orange juice and croissant we get when we arrive.'

'Ooh,' Anne said. 'Yummy. This is going to be fun!'

Julian groaned.

CHAPTER TWO

Introductions at the Hotel Superior

'I'd hate to know what the bloody Hotel *Inferior* looks like,' Julian observed as the cab pulled up outside the day's venue. Despite his low mood, this was not an unfair remark. The hotel had been designed in a somewhat blocky, Soviet aesthetic, and what paint remained on the walls and window frames was in the process of energetically uncurling itself in a bid for freedom.

There were two women on reception. The first fell in love with Timmy at first sight, and brushed away George's excuses for failing to find a kennel for him for the day, saying she'd give him the run of the stables out back. The other lady asked if they were from Finance, Acquisitions or Corporate Relations. It seemed different departments were having team-building days in separate parts of the hotel.

'We're in Acquisitions,' said Julian.

'Ah, then, on the left, please.'

They took their name badges from the table, then made their way down the corridor to a large conference room, where they milled around among many colleagues they did not recognize.

Julian had recovered sufficiently to down the complimentary glass of orange juice and devour his croissant in two bites, while the others stood around, sipping and nibbling. He was still hungry and thirsty, but noticed that the young lady who worked for the hotel was keeping a strict eye on the 'one each' policy. To distract himself, he got Dick to come with him and investigate.

He resented the idea that there were other departments doing team-building in other, possibly much nicer parts of the hotel, and wanted to find out who these other guys thought they were. Sneaking out, they made their way down a lengthy, featureless corridor to the next conference room, and peeped in.

'I'm not sure about this, Julian,' whispered Dick. 'What if we get caught?'

'I'm trying to build your initiative and confidence,' whispered Julian, looking decidedly nervous. 'If we get caught, we'll pretend it's an accident. Oh my *goodness* . . .'

Looking in through the door, Dick wasn't sure what he

'During those team-building exercises this morning, I thought we were going to break up forever and never speak again,' Dick responded.

was looking at for a moment, so he gazed around the room. Then he realized that what Julian was responding to *was* the room. Dick hadn't noticed anything particularly substandard or low-rent about their own conference room, but this was clearly the deluxe option. There was an elevated stage with a proscenium arch at the end of the room; the ceiling was higher and in white plaster, rather than pockmarked, patterned squares; and the floor was parquet, not scuffed carpet.

'*This* is how they treat Corporate Relations?' said Julian. 'If we weren't acquiring things, they'd have nothing to relate to. Or . . . with. Look, they've got bloody bacon rolls for breakfast. I'd kill for a bacon roll right now!'

'Oh, well,' said Dick. 'Time to—'

'Fetch me one.'

'What?'

'You heard: fetch me one!'

'Fetch one your bloody self!'

'Dick, you know very well I'm hungover, so it's the least you could do. Also, I am your line manager and it is an order. *Also*, today is all about building our cohesiveness—'

'Not "cohesion"?'

'Cohesion, building our *cohesion* as a group. And adding

to your skillset is part of this. By ordering you to get me a bacon roll, I am actively improving your CV.'

'Are you, really? I must say, that's very generous.'

'Yes. Finally, never correct my use of language again. I have a degree in English from Oxford University. You knew perfectly well what I meant by "cohesiveness". Consider this a verbal warning.'

Dick wanted to say something back, but instead just sighed wearily.

'Fine, I'll do it myself,' Julian said, marching into the room. Dick chased after, to try and persuade him to come back, but only caught up when they were both at the breakfast table. A pleasant young chap from the hotel began to explain what was available, but, with the vicious selfishness of the hungover, before the lad had finished his sentence, Julian had grabbed a bacon-and-egg roll and was squirting ketchup into it. 'Wizard,' he said, taking an enormous bite.

'Don't know you,' said a friendly bald man of about forty, also selecting a bacon bap. 'What department are you in?'

'Firing people,' said Julian aggressively, through his mouthful. 'I'm really good at it. And what do you do for us?' The man melted away, and Julian took a second gargantuan bite of the bacon roll, leaving only a small corner of it between his forefinger and thumb, and a smear of ketchup at the corner of his mouth.

'Don't turn round,' whispered Dick, standing by his side.

Julian wheeled straight around to see what Dick was talking about. He blinked, taking in what seemed to him a totally anonymous crowd of young-to-middle-aged business people. Then he gasped, and inhaled a mouthful of bacon roll.

'Is he all right?' a woman asked, coming over, after Dick had been thumping Julian on the back for thirty seconds or so.

'He will be, he will be,' said Dick. 'I'll just take him to the Gents, splash some water on his face . . .' He escorted the bent-over Julian out of the hall and down to the lavatories. The second the door closed behind them, Julian straightened at once, instantly recovered.

'Those bastards,' said Julian. 'Trust *them* to come here. Trust them to have a larger conference room than us. With those showy curtains, and the bacon rolls that aren't even *one each*.'

'It does seem like a remarkable coincidence,' Dick admitted.

'They're so smug. I can't stand them. I can't stand to be here, doing a strategy away day, hungover, and, what's more, be in the same bloody hotel as the Secret Seven. I HATE the Secret Seven!'

CHAPTER THREE

Let the Games Begin

'*All* of them?' asked Anne.

'Yup!' said Dick.

'Every last damn one. Lording it over us, with their freshly squeezed grapefruit juice,' said Julian, 'when we've only got orange-from-concentrate.'

'I hate those guys,' said George.

'I'm sure they're nice, really,' said Anne.

'Oh, Anne,' said Julian, 'you're such a pushover. You'd say that about Pol Pot, if you met him. "I'm sure this Killing Fields business must all be blown out of proportion; after all, he had such a nice *face*."'

'Well, I know Peter can be a bit of a pill, and, yes, I'll admit Janet's not entirely my type. But I don't think they're quite in the same league as the Khmer Rouge.'

'My head hurts *so much*,' said Julian.

'Okay, everybody! Could I have your attention, please!' The room went quiet and everyone turned towards the front – which, rather than a built-in stage with a proscenium arch, boasted a shallow wooden platform with an adjustable mic. The deputy head of Acquisitions (south-east) stepped up on to the stage and told the assembled employees how lucky they were to be spending a day '. . . in the company of one of the most exciting new voices within the field of entrepreneurial wellness and conceptual ideation – it's Mr Rupert Kirrin!'

Everyone in the room clapped.

Except for Julian, Anne, George and Dick.

'No,' said Anne.

'Flipping,' said Dick.

'Way,' said George.

'Maybe my brain's melted and this is all a hallucination,' said Julian.

'Greetings,' Rupert Kirrin – the suave, slippery customer who was cousin to all four of them – said smoothly into the mic. 'I'm very glad to be here and to be working with such a dynamic, diverse and exciting group of young professionals. Today, we are going to explore, discover, learn, improve and reshape our very thinking about the business environment. Together, we will take an experiential journey of discovery and renewal – we're going to break everything down to its

'What is THE POINT of all this?'

nuts and bolts, and build it again from the ground up. Our friend is truthfulness, and our enemy is cliché. So I want you to think outside of the box, and give it a hundred and ten per cent. By the end of the day, we will have formed a holistic approach that should really be a paradigm shift for you all . . .'

'Going forward,' muttered Dick to Julian.

'. . . moving forward,' Rupert concluded. He stood back from the microphone and people clapped. Rupert joined in the clapping and stepped forward to the mic again. 'You're really applauding yourselves,' he said, with a voice like treacle, 'because, by the end of today, some things will have changed forever.'

'Well, of *course* they will,' said George. 'That's just the inevitable consequence of time passing.'

'Okay, so we're going to break into our work teams, and there are several exercises for us to do until the morning break at eleven. Then, in the afternoon, we will be outward bound, and extending our learning-and-growing arena into the great beyond! How exciting. If anyone has any questions, please ask me, or, if you can't find me, ask my assistant, Maureen. Say hello, Maureen!' He pointed to a woman of about twenty-five at the side of the stage, who raised her hand reluctantly, with an expression that was equal parts bored and mortified.

With that, Rupert bounded off the stage, and the deputy head of Acquisitions (south-east) came back on to divide the room into groups.

The old adventurers of Kirrin Island were profoundly grateful that, when the room was divided, they were not split up, but allowed to remain in their usual working teams. Soon enough, Cousin Rupert made his way across the floor with a large stack of Post-its in his hand, getting each group up and running with their tasks. He reached their corner of the room last, and before he had a chance to begin, Julian spoke.

'Rupert, what the devil do you think you're doing pretending to be a management expert, or whatever it is you claim to be doing here?'

He should have known better than to expect Rupert to appear abashed or ashamed. Accusations of moral turpitude were, to him, water off a duck's back. 'Julian!' He smiled. 'How delightful to see you. All of you, in fact. Welcome. To answer your question, I am pretending to be nothing at all. I *am*, in fact, a professional motivational speaker and group coherence solution provider, in which capacity, I'm pleased to say, I'm in high demand. Now, here are your packs with itineraries and all the details for later, but, to start the day off, I'm just going to go up and introduce our relaxologist . . .'

In the face of his glossy imperturbability, they all felt a familiar combination of weary acceptance and disappointment as they submitted to the first exercise of the day.

George had felt sorry for Timmy when she had seen him being taken on his own to the stables out the back of the building, but now, if anything, she felt jealous.

CHAPTER FOUR

Starting Out

After the introductory tasks were out of the way, Cousin Rupert disappeared into the background and the stage was taken by a rather dreamy woman wearing a baggy woollen cardigan over a floor-length cotton dress, and many beady necklaces. She instructed everyone in the hall to lie down.

'Now that we've got to know each other a little,' she said, 'we're going to ease into your special day with some relaxation exercises, to make you as receptive as possible. I want you all to close your eyes. And breathe deeply. Breathe in, breathe out. Nice and deep. Nice and deep. In and out.'

'How else are we supposed to breathe?' muttered George.

The woman instructed them all to feel their limbs go limp, as though they were melting into the floor. 'Breathe in,' she repeated, 'breathe out.

'I want you to imagine you are rising out of your bodies. You are floating, like spirits. Up, up through the roof. Up further, until you can see the countryside far below you. You are entering the clouds, and then you are above the clouds . . .'

Anne was concentrating hard on getting this right. She was lying rigid and picturing everything the woman said, anxiously wondering if she was relaxed enough, and whether any managerial person might conceivably notice how well she was performing the exercise.

Dick and George were both already very relaxed, and, by following the instructions, were mellowing to the point of sleep. It was like they were at a spa. Julian, meanwhile, was fighting the woman's suggestions as hard as he could, because they were making his head swim – which only served to make the visions stronger and clearer.

'Swoop down over the placid blue waters of the ocean,' she said. 'Now you are in the ocean, and all you can hear is the song of a whale. Now you approach the whale, and as it sucks in water, you flow into the enormous protective cavern of its belly. Now you are the whale, part of the cycle of life, cresting the waves and breathing out air, then diving again. You feel its memories, its memories of the sea. And now you are the sea . . . Breathe in, breathe out . . .'

*

After this, all found themselves much relaxed – except for Julian, who looked rather green around the gills. Cousin Rupert took the stage and announced the attendees would presently, in their teams, go into various smaller rooms for the morning exercises, before meeting up again at lunchtime.

Once ensconced in their small meeting room, they were introduced to their leader for the morning: a man in his thirties, called Mike. He was tall, shaven headed, bespectacled, clear-eyed and earnest without looking in any way intelligent. Combined with his cheap blue suit and waistcoat, the overall effect was of someone who had given up his dreams of being an actor, but not yet accepted his fate as an estate agent. After shuffling his papers around for a while without meeting their eyes, he abruptly announced that they were ready to proceed.

'No, no,' Julian said. 'We should wait for the rest of my team first.'

'I think this is it,' Mike said, consulting his clipboard. 'Yup,' he confirmed, looking up.

'But my team's twice as large as this,' protested Julian. 'Where are the others?'

'Various things. Adam Quigley is at his grandmother's funeral.'

'The final exercise of the day is about empowering our core competencies.'

'Well, that's a lie. That's the *third* time he's said that.'

'Diana Pilkington phoned from Brighton to say she'd got on the wrong train.'

'Pathetic, although I wouldn't put it past her.'

'Typical Pilko!' said George.

'Nick Mason has to take his two-year-old to the doctor.'

'Two-year-old?' Julian spluttered. 'That man is a classic virgin! You can spot it a mile away!'

'And James Sunday claims to have contracted Creutz-feldt-Jakob disease.'

'That'll be the least of his problems when I get my hands on him,' Julian said. 'What a turn out! This is what they think of me!' He rubbed the bridge of his nose with his eyes scrunched shut.

'Never mind, Jules, old chum,' said Dick, slapping him on the back. 'I bet our chances of winning awards at the end of the day are improved without that lot. They're just baggage.'

'There are *awards*?' said Julian, his hangover forgotten.

'Oh, yes,' said Mike. 'Awards are given in each category for the best-performing teams.'

'Well, in that case, Dick is quite right,' said Julian, visibly relieved. 'That lot are a shower of half-arsed no-hopers. We're much better off without them!'

'That's the spirit,' said George. 'Go, team!'

'Maybe that was a little strong,' said Julian, sitting down with the rest of them. 'Don't repeat that to them, please . . . '

'First off,' said Mike, 'you have to pick a team name. That will be on the board at the end of the day.'

'Oooh, like *The Apprentice*,' said Dick. 'I love it. Me first: Orgazmatron!'

'I'm going to say this now,' said Julian calmly. 'If there are prizes involved, you *will* take this seriously. Or you will expelled from . . . Team . . . Team Sophisticus.'

'Team Sophisti*cuffs* might be more like it,' said George.

'That's quite good, actually!' said Anne.

'Stop, stop,' said Julian. 'Let's write these down . . .'

In the ten minutes that was allotted to the task, they threw out the first suggestions and ended up with a shortlist, some of which Julian thought were good, some he suspected might have been suggested in a spirit of mockery:

Brillopadz
Fabulosity
Excellentia
Dominax
Vibressence

Majestica
Fortissimo
Excelsior
Harmoni-us

'Hard not to sound like a gay club, or a brand of sanitary towel, isn't it?' said George.

'Well, there's one clear winner as far as I'm concerned,' said Julian. 'Excelsior it is.'

Mike, who had been leaning against the wall and apparently dozing, sprang to life. 'So!' he said. 'Team Excelsior. A smaller team than most, with four members.'

'Five members,' said George. 'We also have Timmy.'

Mike looked to Julian. 'He's not on my list. Where is he?'

'He's tied up in the stables,' said George, 'because he's a dog. But he's *definitely* part of the team.'

'Fine,' said Julian, waving a hand.

'Timmy,' said Mike, writing the name down. 'So. On with the first task. This is a Togetherness Exercise, where we build trust, positive thinking, language skills, empathy, cooperation and concentration.' Opening a file, he gave Dick and Anne some red balloons to blow up. Then he walked across the room, placing sheets of paper on the floor, seemingly at random.

'The team leader has to come to the front of the room,' he said when he had finished, 'and put this on and get spun around twice.'

Julian liked being identified as the team leader, and liked being asked to walk to the front. He was not so delighted with the item presented to him. 'I'm feeling rather light-headed,' he said. 'I'm not sure that this is—'

'Bear in mind that I have to mark you each for your individual performance,' Mike said. 'And that contributes to Excelsior's overall score for the day.'

Julian hurriedly put the blindfold on. Mike handed a balloon to each of the others and requested them to stand behind Julian in a conga line.

'Now, Julian is leading you all through the minefield,' Mike said, 'and if he sets foot on a mine, it will go off, killing you all.'

'Come on, team, we can do this,' muttered Julian.

'We're actually here, Julian, behind you,' said Anne.

'Yes,' he said, turning round. 'I knew that.'

'What I need you to do is direct Julian between the mines, to the safe zone at the other end of the minefield.'

'For god's sake, let's have those ciders, that'll cheer us up.'

'Easy peasy,' said Dick.

'Wait. You have to use your linguistic skills very carefully. Because you are not allowed to use words like "left", "right", "forward" or "stop". More importantly, you're not allowed to say anything negative. Every instruction has to be encouraging, or couched in positive terms.'

'*Neasy* peasy,' said George quietly.

'You see,' Mike said, 'it's what we call a metaphor, for your life as a te—'

'Yes, we know what a metaphor is, thank you,' said Julian.

'Okay, good. So, you are at the starting line now, Julian. And . . . go, Team Excelsior!'

Despite having been turned around fast, Julian felt he had a relatively good memory of where the nearest few mines were, and so he took two confident steps forward. He was immediately assailed by a chorus of shouts, and his confidence dissolved.

'I'm not so sure about that, Julian!' yelled Dick.

'Negative comment, there,' said Mike.

'That's a brave move, Julian,' said George quickly, 'but I think I'd re-evaluate your direction.'

'Okay,' he said shakily. 'Then, where?'

There was silence for a moment.

'I think our best collective interests,' said Anne carefully, 'might be served in making a modest move in an easterly direction.'

'Well, then, you'd better give me a braille compass and teach me braille while you're at it!' Julian barked.

'Interesting leadership technique,' he heard Mike mutter somewhere behind him.

'That was a joke, just a joke,' said Julian. 'Sorry. Perhaps it was too aggressive to be funny. I appreciate, now, that I should be more respectful of my team's feelings. I've just learnt that. What a good exercise this is . . .'

'If you don't stop sucking up to Mike, we'll never get out of this minefield,' observed George.

Julian reddened and opened his mouth, thought, and held back what he was about to say with a visible effort. 'Well spoken, George,' he said. 'I respect you more for that. Now, for goodness' sake, where next?'

While they had been engaging in repressed bickering, Dick had perceived a flaw in the rules of the game. 'Julian,' he said. 'If I could suggest a . . . a . . . an *ideation exercise*,' he went on, plucking the phrase out of a list of those he most disliked and assuming, therefore, it made sense in a team-building context. 'May I recommend that you imagine the far wall, where the safe zone is, and where you happen to be pointing, to be north. And therefore those on the sides of the room to be correspondingly east and west?'

'Dick,' said Julian triumphantly, 'I think you are displaying some great team-membership qualities.'

'Well, then,' Dick went on, 'I would suggest it might be wise to take a step to the north-west.'

'Brilliant,' said Julian, striding forward in that direction.

'BOOM!' yelled Mike, as the non-blindfolded members jumped in fright.

'What?' Julian asked. 'What happened?'

'Er, it seems I meant north-east. Sorry,' said Dick.

Julian withdrew his foot. He turned his bandaged eyes to where he imagined Mike to be standing. He let out a ragged breath and wiped sweat from his brow. 'Not to worry, Dick,' he said with chilling calmness. 'It could happen to anyone.'

'Two lives left,' said Mike.

CHAPTER FIVE

Go Excelsior!

'I like the direction you're going with this, Julian,' said Anne. 'But I wonder if a gentle course-correction in the opposite direction might help.'

'I'm grateful for your input,' said Julian.

Twenty minutes had passed, and, after their initial mishap, the team had realized their only chance of success was to proceed by a painstakingly slow and meticulous progress of tiny shuffling steps, each attempted only after dozens of frustratingly vague instructions. However, the clock was ticking down.

Julian had by now sweated through his shirt, and his hands were trembling with a combination of nerves and the last of the Captain Morgan passing out through his pores. This was torture – he had genuinely awoken from nightmares considerably more enjoyable than this game – and, in truth, he had been quite humbled by it. The others were equally nervous at the prospect of Julian's temper if they failed this task, and, to add to the torment, the balloons squeaked constantly in their sweaty hands. After a while, Mike had said that their continuous use of the compass system was stretching the rules and, if they continued, he would report it. They were thrown back on their wits.

'My counsel, if it was deemed welcome,' said Dick, 'would be that, with the last turn, we have drifted into an unsafe arena, and it would be best to turn a ninety-degree angle in the opposite direction, and take a twelve inch step.' Julian made a sequence of four tiny three-inch steps.

'I think that is a remarkable achievement, Julian,' said George. 'And might I suggest that, in this bold and helpful new direction, we have gone far enough? And that, going forward (but not going *forward*, if you see what I mean), an even better course would be to take a right angle back the way you previously turned?'

Julian repeated these instructions under his breath, and wiped a drop of perspiration from the tip of his nose.

'Now, a full step ahead would seem to be in our best interests,' said Anne. *Squeak squeak squeak*, as they all adjusted the balloons, shuffling forward behind him, looking like a doddery caterpillar.

There was a collective intake of breath.

'What?' said Julian. 'What is it?'

'We believe in you,' said Dick, 'as we believe in all of us together, as a team. The final goal seems within sight.'

'Okay,' said Julian. 'Jesus. Okay. Let's not mess this up. Where's the nearest mine?'

'Directly widdershins,' said George.

'I beg your pardon?'

'Widdershins,' George repeated, frustrated. 'It's another name for a word we can't say. The nearest mine is near you . . . to *port*. Or larboard.'

'Port . . .' Julian muttered, trying to remember from his beloved Patrick O'Brian novels which that was.

'Port out, starboard home,' said Anne primly.

'That doesn't bloody . . . I mean, thanks, Anne, for your not-directly-applicable feedback. Which I shall bear in mind. Port . . .' His head swam, and it occurred to him that a glass of port right now would really sort him out.

'Put it this way,' said Dick, 'the greatest danger is if you take a step to the side that, in boxing, you would refer to as "southpaw".'

Julian spluttered. 'Southpaw? Boxing? Dick, you know I deplore blood sports!'

'You know how many unread emails I've got on my work account? Four hundred and eighty nine. So what the bloody festering pig testicles am I doing here?'

George piped up: 'Just one more step. Where the Conservatives sit, but where Labour lies!'

Julian began to sweat freely and the vein at the side of his forehead pulsed as he panicked, and felt the logic of what George had said slip out of his grasp.

'I'm counting down; your time's nearly up,' said Mike.

Anne had a stroke of genius. 'Julian,' she said calmly, over a loud noise from the corridor outside, 'you need to make the chess move of a *queen's knight*.'

'But I don't know what that is either! Is the queen left or right of the k—'

'Oh dear,' said Mike, 'you used those words . . .'

'Oh, for FU—'

'Timmy!' George yelled as the door burst open. 'My darling, dearest, wonderful boy! What are you doing here?'

'Woof!' Timmy wailed unhappily. 'Woof, woof, woof!'

'What have they been doing to you?' George asked, bending down and smothering him with cuddles and kisses.

'That's time up, and it's a fail, I'm sorry to have to say,' Mike said, clicking his stopwatch and regarding his clipboard glassily.

'What do you mean?' roared Julian, ripping his blindfold off, apoplectic at the idea he had gone through that torture in vain. 'Interruption by an animal, surely! We get to go again!'

'Julian trod on one landmine, which is allowed,' said Mike. 'But I'm afraid one teammate has stepped on quite a few more.'

They looked down at the pieces of paper arrayed across the floor, which made for a dismaying sight. Although he'd only been in the room for a few moments, somehow almost every sheet bore the muddy footprints of a certain beloved mongrel dog and teammate.

'Oh, *Timmy*,' said George, kissing his head. 'You've blown us all to smithereens.'

Timmy whined, and hid his tail.

CHAPTER SIX

A Personality Test

George knew (as they all did) that Timmy was not a temperamental or a nervous dog; if he was alarmed, it was for good reason. So, before they could start any new exercise, George took Timmy to find out what had spooked him.

While she was gone, Mike promised the others the next challenge they faced would be a very special and unforgettable one. He said it was going to make them rethink everything they knew, and create a paradigm shift, and really push the needle, but they weren't really listening to him by that point. There was only so much of this stuff you could take in.

George, meanwhile, made her way to the old stables where, not finding any hotel staff to talk to, she let herself in. What she saw inside made for mightily interesting viewing, and she apologized to Timmy again for leaving him there, and then returned with him to reception. The receptionist, hugely fond of dogs, was horrified at the story

George told her. She emphatically insisted how awful she felt about the situation, giving Timmy a kiss on the head herself. She promised to take him personally and tie him safely by the kitchen entrance, give him a bowl of water, and check on him every fifteen minutes.

George returned to the conference room with a thoughtful expression, to find Mike handing out forms. Anne brought her up to speed: the personality tests they had all taken at the workplace a few weeks before, and which they had all clean forgotten about, had in fact been sent away for analysis, and were a key part of today's proceedings. Now, they were being presented with the results.

'We're going to drill down into these statistics,' Mike explained, 'to make a deep dive, and so that, with this exercise, we cover all our bases. We don't want to always feel that we have to go back to the well, and chew our spinach twice.'

Seeing that George seemed to be feeling faint, Dick jumped in. 'What he's saying is that all we've got to do is cover our bases and step up to the plate and so on, and everything will be gravy.'

George flinched as the sheet that was handed to her touched her fingers. And not just because of her horror for hackneyed idioms. She couldn't remember what mood

They could not forget the words that had been said at that morning's personality test session. In each of them, small grievances seethed and bubbled, little gremlins that grew fat and strong.

she had been in when she filled out the form, but the last time she had filled out a questionnaire was in a teen girl's magazine when she was twelve, and she was so disgusted by the outcome, she had vowed never to answer a questionnaire sincerely again. The document in her hands could say anything, so she glanced over it with distrusting aloofness at first, and then with a confused frown.

Oh, no, she thought. They've broken us into types. We've successfully avoided acknowledging this all our lives. This could be disastrous . . .

'Now, you may not remember filling out these questionnaires,' said Mike, 'but they are going to help us, in this next session, to explore our own identities within the workplace, and how we perceive each other. You can see, at the top of your sheet, you've been designated into one of four character types.' Mike turned a fresh page over on the flip chart, and stood ready with his marker pen. 'Let's start with you, Julian. Can you read yours, please?'

'It says I'm a leader.'

'Is that all it says?'

'No, okay. It says I'm a "domineering leader". Don't know why they have to put that bit in. There's only one type of leader, isn't there?'

'Well . . .' Mike tried to find a nice way to reply to this, but couldn't think of one. 'No,' he said at last. 'There are lots of types. You happen to be one who leads from the front and makes lots of the decisions – which can often be a good thing, depending on the context. Can we name some other qualities a domineering leader might have?'

Here we go, thought George.

'Maybe they don't listen?' suggested Dick.

'Maybe,' said Mike.

'Impatient,' George couldn't help putting in. After all, it was true, and she might not have another chance to tell Julian this any time soon.

'They perhaps always think they're right,' suggested Anne.

'I'd say that sounds possible,' said Mike.

'And, even if they turn out to be wrong, they can be slow to acknowledge it,' said Dick.

'Okay, that's good,' said Mike. 'This is helpful, I think. Now, Dick – what does your sheet describe you as?'

'A "follower-on",' said Dick.

'And do you think that's fair?'

Dick thought about it. 'I suppose so,' he said.

'What words would we use to describe a follower-on?' Mike asked.

'Lacking in initiative?' said Julian quickly. 'Or maybe I mean . . . a failure to grasp the nettle, at times?'

'Perhaps.' Mike nodded. 'George?'

'Well, I don't know,' said George. 'Someone who's trying not to make trouble, I suppose.'

Mike nodded.

'I mean that as a *good* thing,' she said. 'I always feel like I make trouble, so I like people who don't.'

'Perhaps one does sort of have to push him a bit to get things done,' Anne said quietly.

'A follower-on, you mean?' Mike asked. 'We're talking about what we think a follower-on is like, not anyone specifically in this room.'

'She's saying "lazy",' Julian put in. 'Frustratingly lazy. The sort of person who wouldn't save themselves in a boat disaster, but would run to the wrong rescue point and end up having to be pulled out of the water.'

'That's a little rich,' said Dick under his breath.

'I think you've made your point, Julian. Now, let's move on,' said Mike, apparently oblivious to the unpleasant tension establishing itself in the room. 'Anne, what does yours say?'

'It says, "team player".'

'That sounds good, doesn't it – a team player?' Mike suggested. 'Someone who's helpful and supportive, an all-round decent person. But this session is about finding out what others think of us. So what other words could we use to describe a team player?'

There was a silence. Dick, George and Julian might be goaded into insulting each other, mildly, but none of them could bring themselves to say a word against Anne. They just didn't feel as though she had it coming. Mike (who had no idea how long the team had known each other) seemed surprised.

'Well, maybe I'll start,' he said. 'Could a team player possibly be a bit predictable?'

But in a good way, the others thought.

'A little unimaginative, perhaps?' This struck a chord with the others.

'Someone who sticks a little too closely to the rules,' Dick said, hoping he sounded dreamlike and theoretical, and avoiding the sharp gaze Anne was directing at him.

'Fails to see the bigger picture, perhaps?' suggested

Julian. 'Could use a bit of perspective and not worry so much about what people think of them?'

'This is all good,' said Mike, making notes on the board as the housemates turned eyes of sharpened hatred upon each other. 'Now, George?'

'It says, "renegade". Sounds pretty good to me.'

'Yet, in a team environment, is a renegade always helpful?' Mike asked.

'No,' said Julian flatly. 'By their very definition, they are frequently unhelpful and go against the wishes of the group.'

'Although we love them very much,' put in Anne meekly.

'Maybe a tad selfish at times,' admitted Dick. 'They can sometimes make fun of . . . of other members, and what the group is doing.'

'Perhaps that is because sometimes what the group is doing is a load of balls?' suggested George.

'It's not impossible,' said Mike, avoiding George's eye, 'that renegades often have their own agenda and can hinder the group. And perhaps it would be good for them to know that.'

'Let's get this straight,' said George. 'I don't care what any of you think of me, because I'm just doing data entry

'Next we're going to do a very special exercise,' said Mike, 'for which we're going to do some role play.'

in this job and I've only worked for the company for two weeks.'

'Classic renegade,' said Mike, making a note.

'You can be rude or nice and it won't make any difference,' George went on, 'because I'll be gone within the month.'

'I really don't think we're winning this!' said Julian. 'It has to be battle stations from now on! We need to be more of a *team*.'

'Well, this session has surely assisted in that. Shall we break for coffee?' George asked Mike. 'I'd love to check on the fifth member of the team, make sure he hasn't fouled himself.'

Mike looked appalled, and gave them his blessing, nodding acquiescence. The group headed straight for the door. George thought she could already make out the distant bark of the team's fifth member.

CHAPTER SEVEN

Communication Skills

'The next exercise is a very special one,' said Mike, leading them out of the room where the coffee had been served. He was excited, and not just because it was his job to get all this over and done with. It genuinely seemed – despite the clearly very bad mood of everyone around him – that he thought they were going to get a big kick out of what happened next.

George had spent the short break checking on the condition of Timmy, and had missed out on a tea or coffee, returning to see the hot drinks' trolley being wheeled away. The other three members of the team may have taken drinks during the break, but their facial expressions and body language showed no signs of refreshment. Now, they plodded along, refusing to meet each other's eyes.

'A *very* special exercise,' repeated Mike, 'for which we're going to do some role play. Now, seeing as we've offered our comments on our colleagues, this next session is about building our confidence and communication skills. For this exercise, we're going to go outside.'

'I've seen where he's taking us,' said George. 'You guys are *not* going to believe this.'

Mike led them out through a door at the rear of the hotel, across the garden, to two facing rows of stables, which must have belonged to the original building that preceded the current hotel. There were other teams from the company milling about by different stable doors, talking excitedly, either having just completed the exercise, or about to start. There was no clue from listening to them as to what the task actually entailed.

Mike stopped in front of a stable door and stood with arms akimbo, looking pleased with himself.

'Now, guys, what I want you to imagine is that you are working with a new colleague, who is crucial to your team. This colleague's name is –' he consulted his clipboard and frowned – 'Captain Mustard, and you have to persuade him to perform certain basic tasks.'

Dick and Julian's eyes narrowed, Anne cocked her head on one side and frowned. George took rich enjoyment in the looks of confused speculation on their faces as they wondered whether this was some grown-up version of *Cluedo*.

Mike went to open the stable door with a flourish, but they were distracted by a chorus of clapping from behind them. Turning, they were faced with the sight of Peter from the Secret Seven leading a beautiful chestnut mare out into the cobbled yard. The other six broke into rapturous applause, all smiling widely and cheering.

'Good show, Peter!' Barbara said. 'You're such a clever chap!'

'Oh, it's nothing,' Peter said, patting the horse's neck fondly. 'Polly, here, deserves the real congratulations.'

'Full marks for the Secret Seven, yet again,' said Cousin Rupert, making a note on his clipboard.

'Three cheers for Peter!' yelled James.

'Well, if I wasn't feeling sick already, I would be now,' growled Julian. 'I hate that guy so much.'

'So we're doing horse whispering?' asked Anne. 'Mr Mustard is a horse?'

'There seems to be some sort of mistake,' said Mike, looking in through the doorway.

'Now the name makes much more sense,' said Dick, looking over his shoulder.

'This is a togetherness exercise, where we build trust, empathy, co-operation and concentration.'

In front of them, grunting and snuffling around in the dirty straw, was an enormous muddy pig.

'I wonder how this has happened,' said Mike unhappily. 'I'd better go and ask Rupert what to do . . .'

It turned out there had, indeed, been a mix-up with the farm who rented out their animals by the day. However, they could not possibly send a replacement animal in time, and so, seeing as the other horses were all booked up, it was deemed that the best solution was for Team Excelsior to proceed, as instructed, with Captain Mustard.

Forty-five minutes later, they presented themselves back in front of Mike. They were sweating, tired, dishevelled, and Julian's trousers bore several fresh patches of glistening brown. Now they had finished attempting to interfere with him, Captain Mustard had returned, quite unconcerned, to the corner of his stall.

'I'm afraid I'm going to have to mark you down quite heavily on this task,' said Mike. 'You didn't succeed in getting Captain Mustard to follow any of your instructions.'

'On the contrary,' said George. 'We actually whispered to him to run around squealing and shitting himself, and knocking Julian over. That was what we wanted him to do.'

'That's a shame,' said Mike, 'because your specific tasks were to get him to come to the trough and eat, and then to escort him peacefully from the stable.'

'But this is supposed to be a *horse*-whispering course,' protested Julian. 'There's no such thing as pig whispering.'

'I see where you're coming from, there, Julian,' said Mike, 'but, seeing as neither pigs nor horses understand English, I can't see the difference.'

'But I thought this was supposed to teach us *communication* skills!'

'Seventy-five per cent of all communication is non-verbal,' said Mike. 'Perhaps it is your tone or your body language that you need to work on.'

'To work on?' said Anne. 'For the next time we have to talk to a pig?'

'Just in general,' said Mike. 'I'm afraid I'm finding you rather resistant to new ideas, and I'm going to have to take that into account too . . .'

CHAPTER EIGHT

Well Done, the Secret Seven!

As he led them back into the hotel, Mike announced that they had fifteen minutes to get ready for the afternoon's outward-bound session, which he hoped they were all looking forward to. He asked them to meet with all the other groups in reception in fifteen minutes, and then, thanking them for their efforts in the morning sessions, disappeared.

'Are we really going to go off and do that now?' asked Dick. 'I thought we'd have lunch first.'

The others turned to him with frosty looks.

'What?' he said.

'I really hope you're joking,' said Julian.

This disturbed Dick, so he said immediately, 'Yes, yes, of course I'm joking!'

'I'll see you all back here in fifteen,' said Julian. 'First, I'm going to go and try to clean these trousers . . .'

He found his way to the ground-floor bathroom and

examined the stain on his backside, attempting to clean it with paper towels. This was far from ideal because the towels disintegrated and, what was more, he was worried, by twisting around like this, he could do his back a mischief. He peeped out of the door and saw the corridor outside was totally empty, so he decided to take a risk. He pulled off his shoes and then whipped his trousers off and, removing one sock, dabbed it under the tap. Walking with one damp foot for part of the afternoon was a sacrifice well worth making to avoid looking this foolish in front of everyone. Applying his sock to the affected area, he scrubbed furiously and was beginning to notice, with relief, that the stain was fading, when a nearby sound made him jump.

'Well, well, well,' said a smooth voice. 'Look who I've caught with his pants down.' The door hadn't opened, so Julian swivelled round in panic and found himself eye to eye with Peter, lounging in the doorway of one of the cubicles, eyeing Julian up and down. 'Julian, the admired leader of his happy little troupe. What if they could see you like this?'

'Just mind your own business, won't you, Peter?' he asked. 'And they're called trousers, not pants.'

It was torture. He had genuinely awoken from nightmares more enjoyable than this game.

Peter straightened up and walked over. 'How did the morning session go?' he asked, and started to arrange his own hair in the mirror.

'Smashing. Couldn't have gone better,' Julian said, struggling to put on his sock and retain dignity at the same time. 'We've all learnt a lot.'

'Except for you taking a little tumble, I see. Load of rubbish, these days out, of course,' said Peter, 'but we have to do them in order for senior management to give a fig leaf of respectability to their otherwise pervasive, cynical self-interest. Don't you agree?'

Julian opened his mouth. But it was quite difficult to give a good answer to this while putting on a wet sock, so he closed it again.

'Anyway, good luck, old sport,' said Peter. 'Lot of ground to make up this afternoon, of course, but I'm sure you can do it.' And he slapped him on the shoulder. These two things in conjunction were too much for Julian.

'Take your hands off me, you smug toad,' he said. 'And how the devil do you know how we got on this morning? We could be winning, for all you know.'

'I don't think so,' said Peter. What caused Julian alarm

was that this time he spoke with genuine sympathy. 'There's a leader board, you see.'

'A leader board?'

Dick appeared in the doorway in time. One glance at the body language of both men, and the sight of Julian without his trousers, told him everything he needed to know. 'Peter, please,' he said, 'is this really necessary?'

'It's in the conference room. Although, in your case, I suppose it could be called a loser board.'

'Julian,' Dick advised, 'you probably don't want to see it.'

Julian barged past Dick with a curse and marched into the conference room. Cousin Rupert's assistant, Maureen (whose actual name, as attested to by her name tag, was Marie), had spent the break so far putting all the results into it, and adding up the scores. Top of the list, as expected, was Team Secret Seven. And Team Excelsior, to Julian's fist-biting rage, was indeed at the bottom.

'My!' said Barbara, turning round from examining the board and catching sight of Julian. 'Isn't that taking being bottom to the level of a method actor?'

Dick and Peter weren't far behind, the latter glowing with enjoyment as the other members of his tribe came to stand next to him.

'Nice polka dots,' observed Janet, looking over Barbara's shoulder at Julian's boxer shorts.

Julian only just managed to choke back the response that he hadn't picked them himself, his mother had, and immediately broke out in sweat at what a close escape that had been.

'Seems "Team Excelsior" was a pretty bad misnomer, don't you think?' asked Peter, as Julian grabbed his trousers back from Dick and began scrambling them back on. A crowd was gathering as both entire teams now faced off against each other.

'I always thought of you as the Fatuous Four,' said Barbara.

'*Five*,' said George. 'Timmy's a member. My dog,' she added, when they stared blankly at her.

'Oh, your fifth member's a *dog*,' said Peter. 'How *helpful*.'

George pointed at the youngest three of the Secret Seven. 'You know no one has any idea what you're called, right? What is it – Boris, Shirley and Abdul, or something?'

'Fatuous Five works just as well, now I think of it,' said Barbara.

'Yeah?' asked George, always sharpened by any insult that touched upon the honour of her dear Timmy. 'Well, why don't you call us the Go-Stuff-Yourself Five?'

'That's ENOUGH!' yelled Anne. Everyone froze. 'This is all *very* childish. You, Secret Seven – you're way out in front, winning, and yet you can't help behaving like this. That marks you out as bullies. And you lot,' she said, turning on her brothers and George, 'you definitely ought to know better. I'm ashamed of you. Come with me and we'll get ready for the afternoon session. Julian, follow me; you can finish doing your laces up outside.'

Anne had never spoken to them this way before, and they followed her, feeling utterly chastened.

'I hate him *so* much,' said Julian when they were in the corridor outside.

'That's because he's like you,' said George. 'A domineering leader.'

'TAKE – THAT – BACK,' said Julian.

'If you two don't start behaving, I am going to get a taxi to the station and go straight home,' said Anne. They shut up, and resumed their chastised expressions. 'Okay,' she said. 'We've all got our bags packed for the afternoon session, yes?'

'I still don't understand,' said Dick. 'Are we really not being given lunch before we set out?'

It was not a well-timed remark. They turned towards him with all the displaced aggression of the past five minutes. 'Please, *please* tell me you're joking,' said Julian, with quiet rage.

'Aaargh!' said George, and, grabbing Dick's left wrist, she undid the buttons on his shirt and rolled the sleeve back. 'I even wrote it on your arm! What does that say?' she asked.

Dick blinked in astonishment, for written on the inside of his forearm was the legend, *DON'T FORGET TO BRING THE LUNCH!!!*

Anne was horrified. 'Dick! Don't you wash?'

'So I shower in the dark,' he said distractedly. 'It doesn't make me a pervert. The light hurts my eyes when I've just woken up.'

'I take it from this that you have forgotten to bring the lunch.'

'No,' Dick said, looking shell-shocked. He now remembered they were supposed to bring ingredients and barbecue their own food at a campfire. And the division of labour meant that, in this case, 'they' meant 'he'.

'First off,' said Mike, 'you have to pick a team name.'
'Hard not to sound like a gay club or a brand of sanitary towel, isn't it?' said George.

'I brought it, all right. I made sure I brought it. You told me not to forget, and I didn't.'

'So where is it?'

'Under our seat on the train.'

CHAPTER NINE

Outward Bound

When all the teams were gathered together in their hiking gear, they were loaded on to a coach and driven into the nearby countryside, and then dropped off one by one at different locations, far away from each other so that their paths would not cross. Before the first team left, Cousin Rupert stood up at the front of the coach and explained.

'This afternoon's challenge,' he said, 'is intended to promote cooperation, team cohesion, initiative, encouragement and interpersonal relationships. It's also supposed to be really rather *fun*. Good luck!'

As the coach pulled away down the lane from them, Julian took out the map and the instructions. First though, he wanted to check on the food situation. All through the coach journey, Julian had made a point of boasting loudly to Anne about the delicious lunch they had prepared for themselves, and how much he was looking forward to eating it. This was to keep the Secret Seven, who were in the seats behind them, quiet. It worked, but the side effect was that they were all now starving.

'Okay, let's have a look at what we've actually got,' said Julian. Dick held open his rucksack, into which he'd pooled all the food everyone else had found in their bags. There was a packet of dry-roasted peanuts, a tube of mints, four cans of cider and a tin of dog food.

'Woof!' said Timmy.

'Yes, you're all right, aren't you?' said Julian bitterly. 'Shall we count out the peanuts?'

'My life has not reached such dire straits that I am reduced to counting out my share of a packet of peanuts,' said George. 'You can have mine.'

'And mine,' said Anne. 'Let's get walking; it'll take our minds off matters, for the time being. Dick, you take the map and the compass; I know what men are like. What are our group objectives?'

'There are several,' Dick said. 'First, we need to hike to a certain point, where there should be a marker for us to collect. Then, we strike camp and build a tent and make a fire. We take a picture of ourselves around the campfire. Finally, we have to find our way back by a different route, and the first team who returns is the victor.'

They had been dropped by a gate. 'Seems like the route takes us through this field,' said Dick, unlocking it and pushing it open.

'Let's get marching!' Julian said, striding ahead in his wellington boots. He was pleased to have the peanuts in his possession and keen to move everyone's attention on to new things, hopefully to make Dick somehow forget about his share as well. He was already able to think of little else other than his hunger, and if he didn't eat, he felt it would get the better of him. He turned, and found the others straggling behind (except for Timmy, who of course raced ahead with his tongue hanging out and his ears flapping).

'Come on!' Julian called. 'We don't want the Smug Seven to win the day, do we?'

The others picked up their pace a bit, but something was clearly bothering them. They wouldn't meet his eye.

'What is it?' he asked.

'I think Anne should lead for a bit,' said Dick.

Julian emitted a strangulated syllable, which was the result of a man trying to repress a snort of derision even as it crossed his lips – a deeply curious noise. He stopped, waited for the others to catch up, then let Anne walk ahead.

'By all means,' Julian said quietly. 'I think it's a good idea. I'm sorry for being so –' he gulped as though swallowing cold tea – 'domineering.'

'Anne, old chap, have a look at the old map and see if you think we're going in the right direcsh,' Dick suggested.

'No, please, thank you, Dick,' said Anne. 'I hate maps, and I take your word for it we have to go this way.'

'Why, thank you, Anne,' said Dick. 'That's nice of you to delegate to me like that. What a nice, trusting leader you are.'

Julian watched carefully as he said this. Dick managed to hide his evident enjoyment and went so far as to start whistling innocently up into the sky. Julian kept watching him for some time, not realizing that George was getting an eyeful of them both and it was making her day.

'Peanut, Dick?' Julian said lightly, tearing open the packet.

Dick looked at him, and the proffered pack. He accepted a few and, after he had swallowed them, some of the glee had gone out of his expression. The whistling stopped.

Fifteen all, my friend, thought Julian. Your serve.

They soon met the gate on the other side of the field, which was too deeply encased in mud to open, so they clambered over it. Dick examined the map again frowningly, but said that, as long as they could cross to the wood on the far side, they should find a stream, with a bridge, where they should turn left.

'Timmy!' called Anne. 'Don't do that. Come here. This is someone's field. Wait until we're in the woods.'

When they reached the other side of the field and climbed over a stile into the woods, there was indeed a stream – more of a four-foot-deep muddy gorge – over which the bridge clearly identified on the map turned out to be a wooden plank that had long ago rotted and snapped.

It was agreed that it was now George's turn to be in charge for a while, and although they expected her to be rather mocking about the enterprise, she embraced the role with unexpected seriousness.

'That looks roughly correct to me,' she said when Dick showed her the map. 'Now, Dick, the enemy seems to have eliminated our bridge over this stream. But we will not let this get in our way, will we?'

'You are floating, like spirits . . .' instructed the relaxologist. Anne anxiously wondered if she was relaxed enough.

'No, I suppose not.'

'"No, I suppose not" what?'

'What?' he asked.

George yelled, 'I said, "No, I suppose not" what? It's "No, I suppose not, *sir*!" Isn't it!'

'We're not in the army, George,' said Julian.

'"We're not in the army, George, *sir*,"' said George. 'Except, on my watch, we *are* in the army. I am the very model of a modern major general! The next person who disrespects me gets ten press-ups!'

'Oh, really, this is too much,' muttered Julian.

George turned on him. She pointed at the dirt. 'Ten,' she said.

'No,' said Julian.

'For the remainder of my duty, no one is to talk to Private Julian,' said George. Julian saw from their downturned eyes that Anne and Dick were going to accept this diktat. Typical, he thought. Typical 'team member' and 'follower-on' behaviour. Risible.

'Now, Dick, jump over that stream to make sure it's possible.'

'Righty-ho,' said Dick. '*Sir*,' he added quickly, saluting. He took two steps and jumped, and despite his supporting foot sliding a bit as he leapt, raising the exciting chance of him landing, face first, in the mud, he made it with room to spare. The other three clapped to mask their disappointment. Dick reached out an arm to hand the others across – except for Timmy, who for the time being had taken up residence in the ditch, where he was licking something revolting-looking. When the others were all across, they called to him and he bounded out, so covered in mud he looked like he was in camouflage. They all set off into the woods.

Here, they should have been in their element. They trudged beneath a dense canopy of green, listening to birdsong. Around them, the undergrowth contained small hurrying things that Timmy chased after like madness. There was so much about this walk – occurring as it was, technically, in the middle of a day at the office – that recalled in a wonderfully unexpected way the summers of their youth.

But they could not forget the words that had been said at that morning's personality-test session. They tried to, but in each of them small grievances seethed and bubbled, little gremlins that grew fat and strong as phrases played repeatedly in their minds. Tension accumulated in the group, until they were like a volcano whose status has silently changed from dormant to active.

Only Timmy, the large muddy hound sprinting around them and fetching sticks, brought them back to the present in an ecstasy of innocence.

CHAPTER TEN

Team Cohesion

'Maybe that should have been our name: Team Cohesion,' said Anne, to break the silence. No one responded, because the other three were all studying the map and frowning. It wasn't one of those maps with subtle shades of meaning that invited different interpretations. None who looked at it could be in any doubt – they were supposed to be walking in a straight line through a wide, flat wood, until they reached a clearing.

They lowered the map and looked again at the medium-sized lake in front of them. Dick (whose turn it now was in charge) squinted at it, hoping it would resolve itself into a mirage, then returned his gaze to the map. He looked uneasily over his shoulder in the direction they had come from, then back at the lake, making calculations. 'I suppose we go round?' he asked.

'Don't ask me, team leader,' said Julian. 'I'm just a follower-on.'

'Right. Then we go round.'

This was easier said than done. Every step of the way so far they had been on some form of path, however rudimentary. Now, they had to trudge through long wet grass (into which one's foot was liable to disappear with a squelching gulp) and over fences topped with barbed wire. Although it seemed manageable enough from where they started, once they started to walk round the thing, it was as if it reshaped itself, so that whichever part of the shore they were traversing was the endless, exhausting bit, while the rest of the lake remained modestly sized, even cute-looking. Tiredness and shortness of temper began to show, but sensing once more that they were falling behind the other teams on the exercise – and under George's strict leadership – they kept up a good pace, despite being fed up.

Realizing that George's rigid military bearing was an effort to be as un-renegade-like as possible, Anne announced that she was going to be the 'renegade' on the team for the rest of the day. This involved being generally surly in response to questions and otherwise doing a rather savage impression of George's rough manners, including the occasional burp. George, for her part, was genuinely hurt by this display and retreated into a rather tight-lipped, buttoned-up silence, which the others all assumed was intended as a parody of Anne. This all made the boys decidedly uncomfortable, and so they trudged onwards, wondering what could have gone wrong with the map, while the pressure beneath the volcano grew.

At long last, they found themselves roughly on the opposite side of the lake. But their spirits dropped again, for even here the terrain didn't correspond to the map. Dick had, by now, long been entertaining dark doubts he did not wish to put into words. Julian looked bleakly across the lake – retreat was hopeless.

'Let's go up this hill at least,' said George. 'See what's on the other side.'

'If you like; I don't care,' said Anne. She hawked and spat.

'For God's sake, let's have those ciders – that'll cheer us up,' said George. Dick dished them out and they cracked them open as they ascended the hill. Peace of a sort descended on them and they threw sticks for Timmy without making any other derogatory remarks to each other until they were almost at the top of the hill. Then they all stopped.

Timmy came running up to them with the stick and dropped it at their feet, panting. 'Woof?' he asked.

'Shhh, Timmy,' George said, patting him. She turned to the others. 'Is that . . . *singing*?'

They kept walking to the crest of the hill, until they could see over. They were expecting a clearing on the top of the hill, but instead it dipped into a rather picturesque hollow, protected by a thick canopy of leaves above and with walls decorated by fat, gnarly roots, straight out of a children's picture book of nursery rhymes.

It was not these things, though, that made them gasp. It was the fire blazing healthily in the centre of the hollow, between two large tents. It was the unblemished, brightly coloured cleanliness of those tents; it was the sight of what looked like several pigeons roasting on a spit over the fire; it was the air of happiness and satisfaction that hung over the camp like mist; it was the sight of seven people sitting in directors' chairs, strumming ukuleles.

'Kum-ba-ya, my Lord, kum-ba-ya,' they sang.

'Kum-ba-ya, my Lord, kum-ba-ya,' they continued.

George stalked towards them through the undergrowth with the focused intensity of a Vietcong guerrilla, her only weapon a biro clenched in both hands.

'By the end of the day we will have formed a holistic approach that should really be a paradigm shift for you all.'

'Kum-ba-ya, my Lord, kum-ba-ya,' they went on, seeing their guests now and beckoning them over.

'Oh, Lord, kum-ba-ya!' they concluded.

'Julian!' Peter called, the firelight flickering in his eyes, and his cheeks ruddy. 'What a special treat to see you again. You chaps are off course, I notice – perhaps you smelt the barbecue and came to see if there was any leftover quail meat. Well, you'll have to wait and see, I'm afraid. Jack's made these marvellous Lebanese flatbreads, and we're making wraps with salsa verde and some radish, pear and celery slaw.'

'*Cole*slaw,' said Julian.

'But what am I thinking?' Peter chuckled at his own forgetfulness. 'You must be stuffed after eating all that delicious food you were telling us about on the coach. I'd gladly offer you a drink instead, but I see you've already got some cans of delicious corner-shop cider on the go. Alcohol not allowed on these outward-bound exercises, don't know if you realized?'

'Well, it's hardly—'

'Oh, don't worry; I shan't tell, if you don't,' Peter said, holding up his martini glass as Barbara offered him the shaker. 'I'll have an olive. *Dirty*, please,' he said with a twitch of the lips, and she giggled.

'I think you'll find it's you who's off course,' said Dick, but with not nearly enough conviction.

'Come on, guys, let's push on; I don't want to disturb the *Jungvolk*; it must be nearly time for their callisthenics,' said Julian.

'*Best* of luck finding your way back in the right direction,' said Barbara.

'Don't try it,' said George, standing over her, 'because I'd win. There's a good girl.'

Janet jumped up to defend her teammate, but George stopped her with a look. 'Sit back down with the other forgettable ones,' she said. 'Betsy, Pedro and Archibald, or whatever they're called.'

'Nice to see you, Anne,' said Peter, as she passed.

'Whatevs,' said Anne, crumpling up her empty cider can and drop-kicking it with her wellington boot, clean over the roofs of both tents.

The five teammates got far away as quickly as possible after that, Timmy the last to retire once he'd been convinced that there were to be no scraps of quail for him.

CHAPTER ELEVEN

Rum Intent

There was no denying that the world outside that hollow was a less cosy and welcoming proposition. The wood quickly thinned out, and then they were on recently tilled fields again. A wind was starting to whip up and the sky had darkened. So focused were they on getting far away from the Secret Seven without further incident that, for a while, they had abandoned the map. From here, however, they had more of a view than they'd been allowed up to now, and so they checked the map to see if they could make out any landmark on it at all.

Ahead of them, about a quarter of a mile away, was a copse of deciduous trees, a barn and a church spire. The map showed none of these things.

'For pity's sake, let's pitch a tent at least,' said Julian. 'Then take a photo of ourselves around it. That's one thing we can achieve. Head over to that copse and do it there, out of this wind.'

This was one thing they could agree on. They made good speed across the field and, when in the copse, set up camp. They took the parts of the tent from its bag and laid them out, then discussed which part was supposed to go where, and who would do which job. They all spoke quietly and politely. No one took the lead and no one delegated, so there was, instead, a protracted sequence of calm discussions, where everyone volunteered to do everything, and no one complained their progress was agonizingly slow (except Timmy, who ran back and forth around them, yapping encouragingly). Anyone watching would have thought that here was a group of people who had never met before.

They managed to get the poles all straightened, and were beginning laboriously to thread them through the holes of the under-sheet when the canvas between them started to make pocking noises, and they saw fat drops of rain landing on it. At first, they were few and far between, one every few seconds or so. But the frequency of the drops began to increase ever so slightly, which filled everyone with foreboding. The group worked as fast as they could, getting things snagged, pulling them back, apologizing, trying again, throwing the top-sheet over before it was ready, then squeezing together to try and bend the poles

'We're going to break everything down to its nuts and bolts, and build it from the ground up. I want you to think outside the box and give 110%.'

so the tent would take shape. But, within seconds, the whole exercise was academic. Without passing through an intermediate phase, the rain went from a scattering of drops to a full-throated downpour, and suddenly they could barely hear each other's instructions.

'Retreat!' called Julian. 'Abort! Fall back!'

They staggered away from the tent, which flumped helplessly to the floor behind them, and ran towards the nearest big dark shape – the barn. They found their way in through a side door and stood there dripping for a few moments.

'Why didn't you push harder?' Julian yelled at Dick. 'I nearly had the pole fixed. Then we could have got the other one in and we'd have been fine.'

Dick was in no mood to be shouted at. 'It wasn't me who was holding the other end, it was Anne,' he said. 'But I don't think that's very helpful of you to say that.'

'Ugh!' Julian threw up his hands. 'So now it's not allowed to point out when someone else is letting the team down . . .'

Dick took a step forward, afraid of what he might be about to do.

'Interesting that nothing's ever your fault,' said George.

'What?' Julian asked. 'What is my fault?'

'Nothing, apparently, ever. At least, you don't think so. Yet you're in charge, and here we are . . .'

Julian looked furiously at her, but forbore to say anything else because, above the rain and thunder from outside, he heard the one sound that had always cut through him like ice: his sister's weeping. It was hard to see in the barn, but he followed the sound until he saw a ladder, and saw Anne climbing up it. He apologized sincerely, but she refused to come down, so he climbed up after her to a hayloft, where it was profoundly dark. He found her eventually and gave her a hug, and then saw the other two had followed them up, George with Timmy in her arms. It was, after all, dry up here and comparatively warm, and there was loose hay to settle down in while the storm passed.

None of them said a word. They had never, as a group, felt so broken up, so isolated from each other, so resentful and upset. They all sat there, hunched and quiet, while the barn roof weathered what sounded like biblical cataracts and hurricanes without. Julian took a deep breath, closed his eyes, and concentrated on making the pulsing red pain that had been behind his eyes all day start to ease off.

'You know how many unread emails I've got on my

work account?' he asked at length. No one replied. 'Four hundred and eighty-nine,' he said. 'So what the *bloody festering pig-testicles* am I doing here? I mean, WHAT'S THE POINT?'

'Sssssh,' whispered Dick urgently, tapping his elbow.

'Great, and now I've got a splinter, too,' said Julian. 'Right in the ball of my th—'

'Oh, Julian, do *shut up* for a second and listen,' whispered George.

'. . . No results, no money,' said a voice, hard to make out over the sound of rain.

'There'll *be* results,' said a smooth voice in response. 'By the end of the day. Don't worry. I've got it all sorted out.'

'Don't try and give me the old oil, Rupert.'

The housemates, who had all been dozing a moment before, were now wide awake and bent over, listening intently. The rain seemed to slacken off slightly just at that moment, and the voices became more distinct.

'I need to know where Lupiter Fünckstein are planning to build their new UK headquarters,' the first man went on, 'because, wherever that is, my people are going to get in there and buy it up fast. We know that they're poised to make a bid on the freehold in the next few days, so they *have* to know tonight. We're Lupiter's chief rivals in the European mainland, see, and we're determined to block them out of the UK market. Even if it means industrial sabotage. Billions may be at stake!'

'I know all that stuff. Why are you telling me again? Are you trying to impress the cows?'

'There are cows in here? I hate cows,' the other man said nervously.

'Use your nostrils, dear boy; what do you think this place is used for?'

'Well, the storm seems to be passing, so I think I'll go. But don't forget – it has to be tonight!'

'Yes, yes,' said Rupert impatiently to the retreating figure. 'You just be ready with the money!'

Julian, Anne, George, Dick and Timmy all peeped down at their Cousin Rupert as he lit a cheroot, leaning in the doorway as his fellow conspirator darted out into the rain.

'Creep,' he muttered. 'As though *I* could fail.' Then, chuckling, he turned up his collar, adjusted his hat and strode off in the opposite direction to his accomplice.

'Did you hear that?' Anne turned to the others, her tears forgotten, looking thrilled to her core.

‘Oh, I better than heard it,’ said Dick, holding up his smartphone. ‘I recorded the bastard!’

‘I’m going to punch his lights out,’ said Julian.

‘Wait. I think I’ve got an idea,’ said George. ‘And, with the help of you lot, it might just turn into a plan . . .’

CHAPTER TWELVE

Without a Map

Team Excelsior climbed down and exited the barn with a renewed urgency and sense of purpose. They gathered up the sodden remains of the tent and packed it away as fast as possible before setting out. Their smartphones were picking up no signal and the map (which was entirely useless, anyway) had dissolved in Dick's pocket. So, in the absence of anyone to ask, they simply struck out in the direction they felt was probably the right one.

They passed the church and were about to step out on to the road when Anne said, 'Wait. What's this?' There was a yellow flag tied to the gate. 'The marker we were told to look out for was supposed to be a golden flag, wasn't it?'

'Well, yes, but this can't be ours; we're miles off course. It must be the marker for some other team.'

'Who, do you think?' Anne asked.

George shushed them. 'Is that the sound of approaching ukuleles I hear?'

'Grab it!' said Julian. Dick did so, and they ran as fast as they could down the country lane.

By the time they considered it safe to stop running, Julian was panting and looking exhausted. He was entering the final gruelling stages of the hangover before the plateau of enlightenment, and running in sodden clothes while carrying a backpack wasn't helping (or was helping, depending on the way you looked at it).

'Dick, give me one of those mints,' he gasped. 'I'm starving.'

'I think I can do one better than that, old chap,' said Dick, who was a dozen paces ahead. 'We've struck gold!'

Julian looked up at the sign Dick was pointing at. He tottered somewhat self-consciously, thinking of Peter O'Toole coming out of the desert. It was a stagger that he hoped conveyed immense suffering, superhuman endurance, dignity and majesty of spirit. The sign above him bore a picture of a smiling ewe swathed in a Union Jack. *Lamb and Flag – Free House*, declared the legend beneath it. The countryside seemed to swim around him.

'I'm not sure that's a good idea,' said Anne. 'Shouldn't we get back?'

'To start the day off, I'm just going to go up and introduce our relaxologist...'

'Dearest, darlingest Anne,' said Dick, who always used simpering baby-speak to hide his irritation with her, 'we don't know where we are. Let's go and dry out for ten minutes and see if there's a local taxi service.'

'Anne,' said George, 'get your purse out and go and be a domineering leader at the bar while I tie Timmy up. Mine's a Guinness.'

It had been a quiet afternoon in the Lamb and Flag, which meant the landlady was pleased to serve this rain-drenched and decidedly polite bunch, who presently tumbled in through the door. She could go several better than a taxi service: she also had a warm fire, a selection of home-made pasties and pork pies, some delicious local session ales, and a dog bowl in which George could serve Timmy his lunch.

'I bloody love you,' Dick told the landlady, as he was handed his second pint. She chuckled.

'And is that a home-made Scotch egg?' asked Julian. 'Yes, please! That would be *quallo*. Yum. Do you take cards? Dick, she doesn't take cards; can you sort this out?'

'No time for drinking,' said George, striding back into the bar. 'Come into the garden and look what I've just found.'

Anne, just that moment, hung up calling for a taxi and followed the others.

'*Et voila*!' said George, pointing into the garden.

'Why've you got a tent in your pub garden?' Dick asked the landlady. She explained it was her nephew's, that he'd had a row with his wife and there had been nowhere else for him to go last night, so he'd slept out there.

'Do you mind if we sit around it and take a photograph?' George asked. 'It's for a joke.'

'Go ahead; see if I care,' the landlady said.

They rushed outside, placed their bags around the tent and then Julian, George and Anne sat and ate the remains of their pasties, trying to look as though they were in the middle of a wood, enjoying a fulfilling afternoon's orienteering. Dick angled the camera to keep the garden fence out of sight.

'That's good,' said Dick. 'Good. One more. That's nice, Anne. You're loving this afternoon out. You're the best team ever. You're chatting. Just relax a bit more, George; more natural. That's it. Smile a bit more? Now, perhaps one where you're laughing uproariously?'

They did as he requested, with the immediate response of a zipping noise and a red-faced man sticking his head out of the tent.

'I dunno oo you are, but would you all please SOD OFF!' he yelled.

They all scrambled back inside, whereupon they were told their cab had arrived. Dick and Julian downed their second pints, told the landlady that they would never, *ever* forget her, and squeezed into the taxi with the others. Julian commented that he was starting to feel like something approaching a human being.

CHAPTER THIRTEEN

Make or Break

'The final exercise of the day,' said Cousin Rupert to the reassembled group in the conference hall, 'is about empowering our core competencies. Not just that, but purging and purifying; it's about letting go of the stress of obligation, and leaving things behind. It gives you a chance to go out of today feeling – as I hope you do feel – that you have grown; that you have discovered more about you and those around you; that you are a better, stronger person; that you are part of a greater team.'

Normally, if anyone was giving such a speech (especially Cousin Rupert), Anne would automatically cast a look towards Julian, in case he was smirking, and be ready to elbow him to stop it. But not now. They stood as a team, both rigid and solemn, to all intents and purposes like recruits in whose hearts the zeal for their job had been rekindled to a blaze. Across the room, slips of paper were being handed out to everyone. Julian and the others took

'These questionnaires are going to help us explore our own identities within the workplace, and how we perceive each other,' said Mike.

theirs from Rupert's beleaguered assistant, Marie, who for some reason Rupert was still referring to as Maureen.

'Has everyone got one? Okay. On this piece of paper,' Rupert said, 'I want you to write the deepest secret that you have to keep in your job. The one thing you're not allowed to tell anyone, and that weighs on you, and perhaps sometimes stops you sleeping. Now,' he chuckled into the microphone, 'you don't need to worry what you write. In ten minutes, we're going to take the box, with all these messages in it, and burn it outside, and then watch the flames. That's the purging process and the last part of the day. Everyone ready? Now, write!'

'I say, Rupert,' said Julian rather uncertainly, catching his cousin's arm as he went past, 'this is entirely safe, isn't it? Secure, I mean?'

'This exercise? Yes, of course. Why do you ask?'

'It's just me and my team have been burdened with rather a high-up piece of info on the project I've been working on. I've really impressed upon them how secret it is – it rather weighs on me, truth be told. But it's highly sensitive. Just so I know you're sure this won't get into the wrong hands?' Julian saw in Rupert's eyes that he was half impatient with Julian's earnest do-gooder attitude, and half intrigued. He squeezed Rupert's elbow and leant a little closer. 'It really is a *proper* secret. By which I mean, many others in the company *think* they know the truth of it, but in fact only my team does know the actual location. It's all to do with moving our offices, but you don't care about that. Keeping it secret has been quite a big deal for the high-ups.'

Rupert's eyes flashed, and he murmured understandingly. 'This is to help *you*, Julian,' he said. 'The company's put this on to help you. So you go ahead and write that down, and then we'll burn it in the bonfire later and you'll feel relieved of that responsibility. Does that sound good?'

'It's *safe*, then?' Julian asked, looking at him closely.

'Perfectly.'

Julian shut his eyes and nodded, and Rupert went on his way.

Anne, Dick, George and Julian watched closely as the folded-up papers were gathered into bags that were tied shut before being taken up on stage and placed in a large wooden crate. The crate was then levered up and outside by two men, who went off, stage right, before reappearing on the other side of the window.

'That's where they did the switch,' said George. 'Easy as pie.'

The French windows were opened and everyone came out on to the huge balcony outside the conference room to watch the box being ceremonially set aflame. Then, as the flames rose into the darkening sky, Rupert said a few words of thanks and that he hoped everyone had got a great deal out of the day, that there was champagne being handed round, and everyone could look forward to the prize-giving in an hour or so. He excused himself.

The housemates accepted glasses of what was, in fact, Prosecco (much to the satisfaction of Anne, Dick and George, who all preferred it to champagne) from the circulating waiters, along with some salmon and cream cheese puffs, and drifted over to the balcony edge to watch the hotel health-and-safety man rather hysterically put out the fire with a foam extinguisher. Then they drifted among their colleagues, smiling and nodding, and saying very little.

At last, their vigil was ended, as a hand clasped George upon the back and a gruff voice said, 'Young man, I owe you a huge debt of thanks.' He jumped a bit when he saw George was female, but recovered quickly when he saw she wasn't in the slightest bit offended. Taking the housemates off to one side, he introduced himself as Martin Zaltzwick,

UK head of Lupiter Fünckstein, and got quickly down to business.

'You were right,' he said. 'This was a very crucial bit of news that you gave me this afternoon, about Rupert's betrayal. What's more, I couldn't have come up with a solution in time, and you guys thought on your feet, came up with a plan and saved my bacon. It seems, for the time being, Rupert's swallowed it. In fact, I've just been told he's already left the building, on his way to meet his contact. He's taking the false information you gave him, which they will presumably act on. I don't know how to express my gratitude.'

'I can think of a way,' said Julian, casting his eyes towards the scoreboard.

'Ah, yes,' said Mr Zaltzwick. 'You struggled early on in the day, but you made some good late gains . . .'

'I was thinking we could be given a twenty-point bonus, for services rendered. I'm not saying you have to tell everyone what we did – we'd rather not, to be honest – but perhaps if we found another explanation?'

'No sooner said than done,' said Mr Zaltzwick, who immediately made his way to the podium to announce the bonus award to Team Excelsior for their extraordinary bravery and teamwork in doing the company a special service, and left it at that.

'Where *are* the Secret Seven?' asked Anne. 'Why on earth haven't they returned yet?'

'So stubborn-minded, I could imagine they're still looking for the marker we stole,' said Dick.

'And because they'll never find it, they'll live out there forever, until they get eaten by badgers in their old age . . . ?'

'Sounds good to me,' said Julian. 'If they don't come back, that disqualifies them and leaves us top!'

'Jules,' said George, 'leaving aside how atrociously we've gone about team-building today, not to mention all the exercises we've fouled up, I don't want to stick around here in these soggy clothes and wait to be given a pointless award we'll only have to lug home, anyway. Especially not while my cousin is simultaneously being arrested, and seven innocent acquaintances are unaccounted for in the wild because of my behaviour. It's the winning that counts; let's not stick around for the ceremony?'

'Well, when you put it like that . . .' said Julian.

CHAPTER FOURTEEN

The Ride Home

'So, Julian, do you think we're a better team after today?' asked Anne on the train.

'I think that we get better and better together as a team every day,' Julian said. 'And every day I spend with you guys, I love you more. *Especially* you, Timmy.'

'Woof!' agreed Timmy.

'That said,' Julian went on, 'during those team-building exercises this morning, I thought we were going to break up forever and never speak again.'

'I think we're better,' said Dick. Everyone waited for him to follow it up. 'I just think that we're *better*,' he repeated.

'We'll be home soon,' said Julian contentedly, 'and with a bottle of beer and some leftover lasagne, a comfy chair, and the feeling of having done the right thing. Can anything be better?' he asked. 'I'll tell you: no, it can't.'

At that moment, the train slowed to a gentle lope through an English countryside rendered featureless by dusky

Ahead of them about a quarter of a mile away was a copse of deciduous trees, a barn and a church spire. The map showed none of these things.

half-light. Despite being in the aisle seat, Julian couldn't help but get a good look at the fuss that was going on by the side of the tracks, which they all now realized must be the reason for the train's deceleration.

It certainly made for a remarkable sight. In the evening semi-darkness, a slew of police cars were gathered in a rough semicircle, their headlights illuminating a figure in the centre. He seemed a bedraggled fellow, in tattered clothes, with long dark hair and a long beard. There were chains around his ankles and wrists, and his tatty overalls seemed to have a pattern that was vaguely familiar. The faint ghost of recognition and fear stirred in Julian's head.

'I think that's Carlos the Puma,' he whispered to the others. 'The most famous and diabolical terrorist on the globe today.'

'But he was supposed to have died in that plane crash in Mexico!' said Dick. 'He must have been hiding in these woods all this time!' As they watched, the grizzled master-criminal was hoisted up into the back of a van.

'Who could have found him here, of all places?' gasped Anne. 'It's incredible!'

As the train slowly trundled past, out there in the dark, among the policemen and Interpol agents, Julian caught sight of a familiar figure sitting up on the bonnet of a police superintendent's Bentley, looking deeply relaxed. Away on one side, officers were unpacking crates of small items from which they seemed to be recovering kilo after kilo of smuggled cocaine. It was just a fleeting glimpse, and hard to make out, but Julian could almost have sworn that these items were . . . ukuleles.

No, he thought, it can't be.

And then Peter's face was illuminated as Barbara, next to him, held up a match to light his cigar.